THE SEVEN AND THE MAGICIAN

Enjoy a new mystery for the Secret Seven. They are Peter, Janet, Pam, Colin, George, Jack, Barbara and, of course, Scamper the spaniel.

It's not every day that a new boy at school claims to be a magician, so when Django Papiropesco arrives, the Secret Seven are eager to make friends and discover more. Can Django really make the Big Wheel at the fairground stop at his command, and is he able to appear in three places at once? Is he really what he seems – or just a fraud?

The Seven and the Magician

A new adventure of the
characters created by
Enid Blyton, told by Evelyne
Lallemand, translated by
Anthea Bell

Illustrated by Maureen Bradley

KNIGHT BOOKS
Hodder and Stoughton

Copyright © Librairie Hachette 1977

First published in France as *Les Sept et le Magicien*

English language translation copyright © Hodder
and Stoughton Ltd 1984
Illustrations copyright © Hodder and
Stoughton Ltd 1984

First published in Great Britain by Knight Books 1984
Second impression 1984

British Library C.I.P.

Lallemand, Evelyne
   The Seven and the magician.—(Knight books)
   I. Title   II. Blyton, Enid   III. Bradley,
   Maureen   IV. Les Sept et le magicien. *English*
   843'.914[J]   PZ7

ISBN 0 340 35238 8

Printed and bound in Great Britain for Hodder and
Stoughton Paperbacks, a division of Hodder and
Stoughton Ltd., Mill Road, Dunton Green,
Sevenoaks, Kent (Editorial Office: 47 Bedford
Square, London, WC1 3DP) by Hunt Barnard
Printing Ltd., Aylesbury, Bucks.

CONTENTS

Chapter One

A NEW BOY AT SCHOOL

The door of Peter and Jack's classroom opened, and in came Mr Denison, the deputy headmaster. There was a boy with him – an unusual-looking boy. He had tanned skin, very dark hair, and bright green eyes.

Mr Martin the maths master, who was giving the class a geometry lesson, stopped teaching so that Mr Denison could speak to the boys. There was a murmur of interest in the classroom.

'A new boy!' Peter whispered to Jack, who was sitting next to him. They were the only two members of the Secret Seven Society who were in this class.

'Silence please, everyone!' said Mr Denison. Then he introduced the new boy. 'This is Django Papiropesco. I expect some of us may have a bit of difficulty spelling your name at first, Django! Would you mind telling us where your family comes from?'

The boy gave a wide smile and said, 'Well, my father's family came from Greece and from Hungary in the first place – that was years and years ago – but my mother is English.'

'Well, boys,' said Mr Denison to the class, 'Django is going to come to school here for the rest of this term, and I'm sure you'll make him welcome.'

Then he apologised to Mr Martin for interrupting the lesson, and went out.

'There's an empty desk at the back of the room, Django,' said Mr Martin. 'You can sit there. We'll start the problem again, so that you can catch up.'

The new boy walked across the classroom. Everybody was watching him with interest. He didn't seem to be taking any notice of that. He held his head very high as he went to his desk.

'I say, his clothes are unusual. I rather like them,' said Jack.

'Maybe he likes tinkering about with car engines and so on,' suggested Peter – because the boy wasn't wearing jeans and a shirt or T-shirt, like the rest of them, but a boiler suit like the kind a garage mechanic wears, only Django's was rather a smart boiler suit!

Once he was sitting down, he put his hands in the pockets of the boiler suit and brought out lots of pens, pencils, rulers and an exercise book – all the things he would need for the geometry lesson.

A couple of rows in front of him, Jack and Peter kept turning round to look at the new boy. They wanted to know more about him.

Luckily for them, it was break as soon as the lesson was over. They went straight up to Django.

'Hallo!' said Jack. 'I say – how do you think you'll like coming to school in a quiet country place like this? Will you be homesick?'

So far, Django hadn't been very talkative, but that made him laugh.

'What's the joke?' asked Jack in surprise.

'Oh, just the idea of me being homesick!' explained Django. 'You see, we keep travelling round the country, so I don't know what it's *like* to be homesick! My father's working on the new main road they're building near here, and this'll be the tenth school I've been to this year!'

'Oh, aren't you lucky!' said Jack enviously. 'I'd love to travel round and keep going to different schools!'

Peter decided he ought to stick up for their village. 'Travelling's all very well,' he said, 'but lots of exciting things happen here too, you know! My friends and I have a society called the Secret Seven, and you'd be amazed by some of the adventures we've had and the mysteries we've solved. Maybe we *do* live out in the country – but we have a really wizard time!'

'Do you?' said the boy, laughing for some reason Jack and Peter couldn't understand. 'A wizard time? Well, that's *right* up my street!'

'Whatever do you mean?' asked the two friends.

'I mean,' said Django mysteriously, 'that I'm a magician!'

'He said he was a *magician*?' asked Barbara, astonished.

'A magician?' repeated George.

'He can't be!' said Colin firmly. 'There's no such thing, not outside story-books. He didn't really mean it.'

'He *seemed* to mean it,' Peter told the others. 'Anyway, you can judge for yourselves. He'll be here any moment now!'

'You mean to say you gave him the password, Peter?' exclaimed Pam and Janet together. They didn't look at all pleased!

Peter felt rather embarrassed. As head of the Secret Seven, *he* was usually very strict about not letting anyone outside the Society know their special passwords.

'Peter was quite right to do it,' said Jack, coming to his friend's aid. 'Django seemed awfully interested in our Society – and he said he'd show us some of his magic!'

Tap, tap.

Someone was knocking softly on the door of the shed at the end of Peter and Janet's garden, where the Seven held their meetings. The children held their breath. Scamper the spaniel, who was lying at their feet, pricked up his ears.

'Password?' asked Peter.

'Sausages and mash!' someone said in a clear voice.

'That's him all right!' Jack whispered to the others.

Peter went to the door and opened it, and there stood Django. There was not much light in the shed, and in the dimness his green eyes seemed to glow and his hair looked darker than ever.

He came in. Peter closed the door and introduced the others to him.

'This is a full meeting of the Secret Seven Society,' he told Django. 'You've met Jack already – this is our treasurer, George, and Colin, Barbara, Pam, and my sister Janet. We were expecting you! You can sit on one of these boxes.'

'Woof! Woof!' barked Scamper.

'Oh, Scamper – Peter forgot to introduce *you*!' cried Janet. 'This is our golden spaniel Scamper,' she told Django.

The boy put out his hand and patted the dog. Scamper wagged his tail.

'Look, he's taken to you already!' said Peter, grinning. 'That's a good sign, if we're going to be friends!'

These words made Django's eyes light up. '*Are* we going to be friends? I'd like that!' he said. 'You see, it isn't very easy to make real friends when you're travelling round all the time – and because of my father's job, we're usually leaving places before I've had time to get to know anybody new. It's jolly nice of you to ask me here straight away like this. Oh, I *am* going to enjoy being friends with you!'

Poor Django! Fancy never staying anywhere long enough to make friends! The children felt quite sorry for him, and most of them were thinking it would be a good idea to make him an honorary member of the Secret Society. It wasn't as if he'd be there for good, so it wouldn't matter if the Seven were eight instead, just for a little while.

The girls had taken to Django as soon as they met him. They thought he was very good-looking. George liked him too, and of course it had been Peter and Jack's idea to ask him to the meeting.

But Colin was still not quite sure he wanted to be friends. He was feeling a bit huffy about Peter telling Django the password. Peter would have been very angry with *him*, he thought, if he'd done any such thing . . . no, he wasn't going to take Django on trust just yet!

Now that they all knew each other, however, Peter came to the important business of the meeting.

'I say, Django,' he said, 'how about this magic of yours?'

Chapter Two

MAGIC

'Magic? Oh yes!' said Django. 'Did Peter and Jack tell you I'm a magician?' he asked the others. 'They thought you'd like to see what I can do!'

'Oh yes!' cried Pam. 'Could you turn Scamper into a . . . a fish slice, or something?'

'Woof! Woof!' the poor spaniel protested.

Django and the Seven burst out laughing, and Pam picked Scamper up to pat him and comfort him.

'I'm not a wicked sorcerer out of a fairy-tale, you know!' said Django. 'Don't worry, Scamper. I wouldn't *dream* of turning you into a fish slice!'

'Do you do card tricks, or what?' asked George.

'No, I don't do card tricks either,' Django told him.

'What sort of a magician *are* you, then?' asked Colin. He was beginning to get impatient with all this talk.

'Well, if you're going to understand that, you have to know the difference between ordinary conjuring tricks, which are all a matter of sleight-of-hand, and illusionism or *real* magic!' said Django.

Janet and Barbara looked at each other. *They* didn't understand it at all!

14

'Look – I'll give you an example,' Django went on.

He took a ten-pence coin out of one of the pockets of his boiler suit.

'See this coin?' he said. 'I put it in my right hand, like this. I close my hand over it, and I ask, "Coin, where are you? Where have you gone?" I open my right hand – and it's empty. The coin has disappeared!'

So it had, too! Pam couldn't help clapping.

Django came over to her, and gently pinched the tip of her nose with his left hand.

'Oh, *there* it is!' he said. 'So *you* were hiding it from me, were you, you naughty girl?'

And to her amazement, Pam saw Django pluck the coin out of the air at the end of her nose.

'Oh, well done!' said George and Janet, laughing.

'How *did* you do it?' Colin asked. He wasn't as ready to applaud as the others.

'I made you *think* I was putting the coin in my right hand,' Django told them, 'but it really stayed in my left hand the whole time! So I could easily make it reappear from my left hand anywhere I wanted. That's what's called sleight-of-hand!'

'You're awfully good at it!' said Peter. He was trying to do the same thing with a coin himself – it wasn't as easy as it sounded when Django described it. 'Now tell us about the other sort of magic – what did you say it was called?'

'Illusionism, or real magic,' Django told him. 'You see that whitewashed wall over there? Now if I could make an open window seem to appear on that wall, with blue sky and green meadows and fields of golden corn beyond it, and if I could make you feel sure you heard church bells ringing in the distance, and you thought a bird came to perch on the window sill and sang a lovely song . . . well, if I could do that, I'd be a very good magician indeed!'

'Oh . . . you mean you *can't* do it?' asked Janet, sounding very disappointed. 'Don't you know how?'

Django smiled at her. He looked amused. 'No,' he said, 'not yet. I've still got a lot to learn – but I *am* learning, and I'm sure I'll be able to do all that some day!'

The Seven sat in silence for a moment, thinking of the picture Django had *almost* conjured up before their eyes. It had begun to seem quite real to Peter,

Jack and George. Pam had *nearly* caught the sound of church bells in the distance – and Barbara didn't like to move, for fear of scaring the bird away!

But Colin wasn't under Django's spell at all. However hard he looked at the whitewashed wall of the shed, all he saw was a whitewashed wall!

'Maybe you'll be able to do it and maybe you won't,' he said in a rather sharp voice. 'A colour television programme without any television set or aerial, I suppose. But while you're waiting to master the art of all that, what *can* you actually do?'

The three girls looked at Colin quite indignantly. He had torn them away from the dreamland picture Django put into their heads!

'Honestly, Colin, how can you be so down-to-earth?' said Pam crossly.

'Because nobody's ever invited me to be an astronaut!' grinned Colin.

Pam gave him a nasty look – but luckily Peter interrupted their quarrel before it could go any further.

'I hope you *will* learn how to make that window appear some day,' he told Django. 'It must be hard work doing that sort of thing. But *can* you actually work any magic at the moment?'

Django had been looking rather upset by what Colin said, and now he turned eagerly to Peter.

'Oh yes!' he said. 'I can show you *lots* of things to prove my magic powers! How many proofs do you want?'

'Seven!' said Colin at once. 'There are seven of us, so you ought to give us seven proofs.'

Django ran a hand through his dark hair. 'Seven? That's rather a lot!' he said. But it was obvious that his magician's pride was at stake. 'You asked for seven, and you shall have seven! Here's my first suggestion,' he told the Seven, after thinking for a moment. 'I expect you know about the big Midsummer Fair on the Common? It opens on Saturday. We'll go to the fair together, and as we go up to the Big Wheel it will stop. It'll stop just before we get there. I'll make it go wrong by my magic!'

'Ooh – will you really?' gasped the girls.

Colin couldn't help smiling.

'Don't you believe me?' Django asked him. 'Well, you soon will! Just wait until Saturday. We'll meet outside the entrance to the fair!'

Chapter Three

THE BIG WHEEL

All the Seven turned up for the Midsummer Fair on Saturday. They met at three o'clock on the Common, just outside the entrance to the fair.

The Common was a big stretch of grass, and the fairground people had put up lots of stalls and roundabouts and swings. There was a Big Wheel too, and dodgem cars, and all sorts of other exciting things to ride on. The local people always looked forward to the fair. The entrance was prettily decorated with streamers and paper flowers.

By the time the Seven arrived there was a big crowd, so they didn't see where Django came from – he was just there in front of them all of a sudden! There certainly *did* seem to be something a little magical about that boy.

'Hallo!' he said. 'Well – now do you want to see my first proof that I can work magic?'

Of course they did! They all followed Django as he walked across the fairground. The Big Wheel was at the far end – you could see it towering above all the stalls and swings and roundabouts.

'It's working perfectly all right now, you see!' Django pointed out. There was so much cheerful noise that he had to shout to make himself heard.

He seemed to be speaking to all the Seven, but he was looking at Colin. It was like a challenge – Django might have been saying, '*You* don't believe me, I know. So we'll see who's right!'

As they passed the dodgems, Jack saw his sister Susie and her friend Binkie having a ride. At least, they weren't actually having a ride, because their car was stuck in a traffic jam. The two little girls had got up on their seats and were shouting at the other people on the dodgems to get out of their way so that their car could start moving again. The Seven couldn't help laughing.

'Thank goodness they're stuck!' said Peter. 'Otherwise they'd have been following us about all afternoon, making nuisances of themselves.'

Susie and Binkie were two real little pests – or so the Seven thought, anyway. Susie was very cross that *she* couldn't be one of the Secret Seven too, and however patiently Jack explained to his sister that there couldn't possibly be more than seven members in a Secret Seven Society, she still wanted to be in it. And to get her own back on the others, she was as annoying to them as she possibly could be!

Meanwhile Colin was keeping an eye on the Big Wheel. He wasn't going to let anything distract his attention from it – and he was sticking close to Django!

Next the Seven passed a candy floss stall, and Peter bought some.

'Hallo, Django, how are you getting on here?' asked the woman selling candy floss.

'Oh – oh, fine, thank you!' said the boy. He seemed to be rather embarrassed, though the others couldn't think why. Then he turned to the Seven and said, 'Come on, then – let's not waste time! Keep watching the Big Wheel!'

He pointed. They were quite close to the Big Wheel now – and it was still going round.

'How does that woman come to know you?' asked Colin. He was walking beside Django. 'Did you go into the fair before we turned up, or what?'

'No, I didn't,' Django told him. 'But I – I met her a few months ago. The fair was at a seaside resort, and my father was working on a road not far away, and I met her son at the school we were going to. He took me to the fair one day – we had a really fine time there!'

There wasn't far to go now before they reached the

Big Wheel. The little cars were going round and round, up to the top of the Wheel and then down again. The children were watching intently.

Django was walking just ahead of them. Only a short way to go now – and then there they were, right beside the Big Wheel, and it was *still* going round!

Colin was just opening his mouth to say so, when there came a loud squealing, clanking sound, and the Big Wheel stopped . . .

The people in the little cars squealed too, in alarm. Some of them were stuck right at the top of the Wheel, and their cars were swaying about. It looked quite frightening. A man came running out of the little ticket office where you paid to go on the Wheel. He was carrying a loudspeaker.

'Don't be afraid!' he shouted up to the 'passengers' on the Big Wheel. 'And whatever you do, don't panic and move about – just keep quite still in your seats up there, and we'll have the Wheel working again in no time!'

Then the man went down under the floor of the Big Wheel. There was already a mechanic in blue overalls there, trying to find out what the trouble could be.

'I say! You *did* stop it!' said Peter. He was very impressed. 'That's amazing!'

Django smiled broadly. He was obviously very pleased with Peter's praise.

'Oh, Django, please get it working again!' Janet begged. 'Those poor people must be so frightened up there!'

'All right,' said Django. 'Just move back a little, or my magic to start the Wheel again won't work.'

The Seven did as he asked them – and as soon as they were away from the Wheel and close to some of the stalls, they heard the machinery begin to go round again. The Big Wheel was working just as it usually did!

'Gosh – you really *are* a magician, Django!' said Pam. 'That's all the proof *I* need!'

'I must say, it was astonishing!' George agreed.

'It may be all the proof *Pam* needs, but you've promised us six *more* proofs,' Colin reminded Django. However, even he had to add, 'Though I must admit you've made a jolly good start!'

Peter and Jack grinned at each other. So Colin was beginning to come round!

Chapter Four

SCAMPER'S PARTY

'Password?' asked Peter.

'Big Wheel!' said whoever had just knocked at the door of the shed.

Peter opened it, and in came Pam, late as usual. She was out of breath!

It was Wednesday, and next Sunday was going to be Scamper's birthday. Every year the Seven had a party on the spaniel's birthday, and invited their parents and some of their friends. They were meeting to discuss the arrangements for the party.

Pam sat down on a box next to Barbara and Janet, and Peter, as head of the Seven, opened the meeting.

'First of all, there's the birthday cake! Will you girls make it again this year?'

'Yes, of course,' said Barbara. 'How many people will there be at the party?'

'About thirty, I should think,' said Peter.

'Then one cake won't be enough, will it?' said Janet. 'I think it would be better to make four or five ordinary-sized cakes instead of one huge big one.'

'All right,' said Peter. 'Now, who's going to organise the things to drink?'

'I don't mind doing that,' said Colin. 'We'll have orange and lemon squash, and milk shakes!'

'And we ought to have a pot of tea for the Mums and Dads if they'd rather,' suggested George. 'Then there'll be something nice for everybody.'

'Fine!' said Peter. 'And Jack and I will see about the sandwiches.'

'Right,' said Jack. 'Let's have egg sandwiches, and cress sandwiches, and jam sandwiches, and honey sandwiches, and chocolate spread sandwiches, and banana sandwiches, and . . .'

'Hang on!' laughed Peter. 'It sounds as if we'd better not eat anything at all for days before, if we're going to have room for all that! And who knows – Django may conjure up some sweets and chocolate too!'

'Oh – did you invite *him* to the party?' asked Colin. He sounded a bit surprised, and not very pleased.

'Yes, I asked him when I saw him at school this morning,' said Peter. 'And what's more, he said he'd give a show to entertain our guests, and part of it would be his second proof to us that he's a magician! That ought to be great fun, don't you think?'

'Oh yes, marvellous!' cried Pam. She was always ready to stick up for Django!

'He wants us to put up a little platform in a corner of the garden,' Peter went on. 'And if we tie a string between two trees we can rig up a curtain, just like a real theatre.'

'Oh yes, and we can put out rows of chairs for the audience too,' cried Janet, full of enthusiasm. 'I say, I *am* looking forward to this party!'

The great day came! After tea, the Seven asked everyone to go into the garden and sit down on the rows of chairs. Gradually the audience fell silent. Susie and Binkie were sitting in the front row, looking at the flowered curtain hanging in front of the little stage. Whatever could be behind it?

The show was about to begin! Janet rang a little bell, and Peter came out in front of the curtain.

'Mothers and fathers and friends!' he announced. 'In a few moments you will see Django Papiropesco perform his magic tricks to entertain you! Django has asked me to make sure nobody interrupts during his performance – he needs complete silence to work his magic. And now, here is the amazing magician DJANGO PAPIROPESCO!'

Peter jumped down from the platform to join Jack and Pam in the front row. George pulled back the curtain – and there was Django!

He was wearing his blue boiler suit, as usual. He bowed to the audience, and shook back the lock of dark hair that fell over his forehead. His green eyes seemed to be glowing with mysterious light in his tanned face.

'Ladies and gentlemen,' he began, 'today is Scamper's birthday! So I thought that as a birthday present, I'd give him a journey to the Land of Magic, far beyond the Moon! What about that, Scamper?'

'Woof! Woof!' barked the spaniel. He was sitting on Jack's lap in the front row.

'Very well, Scamper!' said Django. 'Just come up here on stage – and you shall have an experience you'll never forget!'

Jack got up, put Scamper on the platform beside Django, and went back to his seat.

'Now, Scamper,' said the young magician, 'you are going on a most exciting journey – farther into space than anyone has ever been before, even the astronauts who went to the Moon! I think you need something special to wear!'

He put a little black satin cape covered with gold sequins on the dog's back. The audience all chuckled.

'How handsome you look, Scamper!' said Django. 'Now, I want you to look at me. I'm going to mark the magic sign of the Moon on your forehead.'

He picked up a paintbrush and a little pot of white paint, and painted a shape like the crescent moon between the spaniel's eyes.

'You need to be lighter than air and faster than the wind,' Django went on, 'and so I'm going to give you a magic pink patch on your nose!'

He picked up a box of powder and a bit of cotton wool and dabbed pink powder on Scamper's black muzzle.

'There – now you're ready! Are you excited?'

'Woof! Woof!' barked Scamper. He looked more

puzzled than excited.

Django reached behind the curtain and pulled out a shiny black trunk with gold studs on it. When he opened it, everyone saw that it was lined with blue satin. It looked very grand!

'Here's your luxury spaceship, Scamper,' he said proudly. 'Jump in, and you'll be off to outer space!'

Scamper didn't seem to think much of the idea of outer space and struggled a bit when Django tried to make him get into the trunk. But after a few encouraging shouts from the Seven he decided to co-operate and leapt into the trunk.

'Thank you very much, Scamper!' said Django. He closed the lid of the trunk, and turned a big key in its padlock. 'Have a good trip! And when you come back to us,' he added, mysteriously, 'you will be a new dog entirely!'

Whatever could he mean? How could Scamper change inside that trunk – and how was he going to get out of it? *Would* he ever get out of it again? Janet felt rather frightened. She did love Scamper so much! She sat a little closer to Pam, to make herself feel better.

'Off you go, Scamper,' said Django.

And although he didn't touch the trunk, it went whizzing off very fast, all of its own accord, and disappeared behind the curtain.

'Look, there it goes – it's reached the far end of the garden!' cried Django. Everyone turned round to look the way he was pointing.

'No, higher up!' he said. 'Up in the air – above the trees!'

They craned their necks, trying to catch sight of the flying trunk.

'It's going up and up and up!' cried the magician excitedly. He pointed to the clouds. 'You can hardly see it at all now – it's only a tiny dot! There – and now it's out of sight. It's gone too far for us to be able to see it. It's flying away and away into outer space . . .'

Django had lowered his voice mysteriously. Several of the audience held their breath, hardly daring to move!

'And now – now it's on its way back again!' said Django. His voice grew louder. 'It's coming down from the clouds!'

The spectators craned their necks again, but they

couldn't really see anything.

'It's reached the orchard, and here it comes . . . here it is, safe and sound, back from outer space!'

Sure enough, the trunk came moving out from behind the curtain again and stopped at Django's feet!

'What a wonderful journey for you, Scamper!' said the boy. 'Come along – just as I promised, you're a different dog, and we'd like to know some of the things you've learnt on your travels!'

Django unlocked the trunk and lifted the lid, and Scamper jumped out on the stage.

Well, he *looked* just the same as ever! But looks aren't everything.

'Now that you've learned so much, Scamper,' said Django, 'I think you ought to have a rather grander name! How about Signor Scampiero? Yes, that's a good name. You are now Signor Scampiero! Don't be modest – just show your friends in the audience what a clever dog you are!'

Django rearranged the sequinned cape on the dog's back, and then said, 'Signor Scampiero, will you play the drum for us?'

But Scamper – or Signor Scampiero! – didn't move.

The Seven were watching in suspense.

'Signor *Scampiero*,' said Django, very loud, 'please will you play the drum?'

And then, to the amazement of everyone watching, Scamper stood up on his hind legs and beat the air with his forepaws, just as if he were really beating a drum!

'Jolly good! Well done!' cried the audience, clapping.

'And now,' said Django, 'just take a little walk round the stage, will you?'

Peter and Janet and their parents were very surprised to see Scamper get up on his hind legs and walk all round the stage.

'I'd never have thought Scamper could do tricks like that!' said Janet, in amazement.

'This is quite extraordinary!' her mother kept saying.

'Thank you, Signor Scampiero!' said Django. 'Now that you're back on all fours again, what about doing a little arithmetic? Can you count up to four?'

'Woof! Woof! Woof! Woof!' barked Scamper.

The audience clapped again.

'Now count up to seven, in honour of your friends the Secret Seven!'

'Woof! Woof! Woof! Woof! Woof! Woof! Woof!'

The applause was even louder this time.

'Well done, Signor Scampiero!' said Django. 'Now, let's have a little chat! I want to ask you a few questions. You'll bark once in reply if you mean yes, and twice if you mean no. Do you understand that, Signor Scampiero?'

'Woof!' replied the clever dog.

'Signor Scampiero, is it your birthday today?'

'Woof!'

'Are you very old?'

'Woof!' barked Scamper, hiding his nose between his paws.

'Oh, I don't think you're as old as all that, Signor Scampiero! How many years old *are* you?'

'Woof! Woof! Woof! Woof! Woof!'

'You mean you're five?'

'Woof!'

'That's not really old for a dog, is it, Signor Scampiero?'

Scamper shook his head, as if he meant he wasn't sure! That amused the audience, who all clapped as loud as they could once again.

'Do you want to go on with this conversation, Signor Scampiero?'

'Woof! Woof!'

'You don't! Are you tired?'

'Woof!'

'Would you like to turn back into an ordinary dog again?'

'Woof!' barked the spaniel, very loud.

'Then say goodbye to the audience, and get back into the trunk. You have to make your journey the other way round the Moon to break the magic spell – and when you come back, you'll be the Secret Seven's dear old Scamper again!'

Scamper went to the front of the stage, bent one forepaw and bowed his head, just as if he were bowing to the audience. They gave him another tremendous round of applause! Then he jumped

straight into the trunk. Django closed the lid, locked it, and off it went behind the curtain again. The young magician gave the audience a running commentary on its flight through the air – but though everyone tried to spot it up in the sky, nobody could *quite* manage to see it!

A moment or so later, the trunk was back on stage, and out stepped Scamper looking a bit bewildered.

There was more applause to welcome him, and Janet and Barbara took off his 'costume' and tried to wipe his make-up off his face. But although the girls were petting him and speaking soothingly to him, he seemed worried about something. He kept growling quietly and showing his teeth, and they couldn't get him away from the trunk. He was sniffing it in a very suspicious way! He yapped once or twice, but there was such a buzz of excited conversation that nobody heard him.

The stage was quite crowded now. Pam, Jack, Colin and Peter joined Django, the other two girls and Scamper. Pam was so delighted by Django's performance that she gave him a big hug! Jack and Barbara congratulated their new friend, telling him he'd given a really wonderful entertainment for Scamper's party! Colin couldn't help agreeing – but he pointed out that Django still had to give them five more proofs of his magic powers.

In all the fun, nobody noticed George sitting underneath the raised wooden platform, doubled up in fits of laughter!

Chapter Five

THREE PROOFS AT ONCE

On Monday evening, the Seven held a special meeting in the garden shed. They had a lot to discuss – and most of it was about their new friend Django.

'Things aren't always what they seem!' George said mysteriously, for about the tenth time. 'Things aren't always what they seem!'

'Oh, shut up, George!' said Colin crossly. 'You're getting on my nerves!'

'Can't you explain what you mean, old chap?' Peter asked him.

'Things aren't always what they seem!' said George, and he collapsed into fits of helpless laughter yet again! But he eventually mopped the tears of laughter running down his cheeks, and said, 'All right – I'll explain!'

The others all gathered round to listen.

'That flying trunk never left the platform at all,' he told them. 'Its journey into outer space was all nonsense! Django was taking *you* for a ride – not dear old Scamper!'

'Well, *I* knew it was nonsense all along!' said Colin.

'It certainly didn't sound very likely,' agreed Peter.

'Oh – you mean Scamper never travelled through the air?' asked Janet.

'Of course he didn't!' said George.

Janet looked very disappointed, and so did Pam and Barbara. 'Are you *sure*?' asked Pam.

'Of course I'm sure!' said George. '*I* was pulling the strings to work the trick!' he added, with a grin.

'Look here, I'm tired of all this mystery,' said Peter angrily. 'Have we got to drag it out of you word by word? Tell us what you mean, can't you?'

'All right, then. Well, just before the show Django asked me to help him. He explained what he wanted me to do. I was to stay hidden under the stage during his performance – and at the right moments I was to pull strings coming up through the boards and tied to the trunk. I pulled one way to make it disappear behind the curtain, and I pulled another way to make it come on stage again. And that's what I did – it was easy! So you might say *I'm* the real magician!' he finished proudly.

'I knew it! Django's an impostor – I told you so!' said Colin. 'He tricked you all with his silly stories about windows opening to show wonderful land-scapes and so on. Remember, that candy floss seller at the fair knew him. Don't you think there's something odd about *that*? And now it turns out that his performance with Scamper was all a trick! What's the matter with you all? The Secret Seven wouldn't have stood for this sort of thing in the old days, I can tell you! He's cast a spell on you, that's what he's done!'

'Well, he *must* be a magician then,' said Peter. He felt rather clever to have thought of that reply – but Colin's remarks hurt him. He was head of the Seven, after all, and he didn't like to think anyone could hoax *him*. 'Thanks for the speech, Colin!' he added sarcastically. 'Of course the trunk didn't really fly past the Moon – anyone can tell that. But what about the tricks Scamper did? We saw him play the drum, and count up to seven and five, and tell us his age and all sorts of other things. How do you explain *that*?'

Colin looked crestfallen. He couldn't really find an explanation for that part of Django's performance himself.

'All right, he's got us puzzled for the moment there,' he agreed. 'But once we find out more about his tricks, I bet there'll be some easy way of explaining them.'

'What was that word he used – illusionist?' said Jack. 'Well, why don't we just suppose he's a good illusionist? I'm good at science, George is good at maths, Colin's good at English – Django's good at magic. That's all there is to it!'

'George, did you actually *see* inside that trunk?' Colin went on, sticking to his guns.

'Well, no, Django didn't want me up on the stage. I did see Scamper prowling round it and growling, though, as if there was something peculiar about it.'

Suddenly Barbara jumped up from the box where she was sitting. She looked quite white – as if she'd just seen a ghost.

'Oh, look!' she cried. 'The door!'

And she pointed. Somebody had just slipped a letter underneath it.

Colin ran to the door and flung it open.

'There's nobody there!' he said.

All was quiet in Peter and Janet's garden, outside the shed. There wasn't a breath of wind to shake the tall hollyhocks beside the wall, or a sound to break the evening silence.

The Seven stood in the doorway of the shed, staring at the empty garden.

Peter bent to pick the letter up. In their haste to see who had left it, they had almost forgotten the letter itself! He opened the envelope.

'It's from Django,' he said.

'Talk of the devil and he's sure to appear,' said Colin.

'Don't be so silly, Colin!' snapped Pam.

'Stop quarrelling, you two – let's see what this letter says,' Peter told them, and they all went back into the shed and closed the door behind them.

Next Saturday the Seven all met outside the village hall. Once they had all arrived, Peter divided them up into three groups – Barbara and George, Janet and Colin, and the third group was made up of Jack, Pam, and Peter himself. He was following the instructions Django gave in his letter.

The young magician had promised to give them three proofs at once – and if he could do as he said, it really *would* be magic! Django said he could appear in three different places at the same time – the very same time to the exact second.

Still following Django's instructions, Peter told each group where they were to go.

'Barbara and George, you go to the big oak in Spinney Wood. Janet and Colin are to wait outside the Dog and Duck inn. Jack and Pam and I will ride out to Torling Castle on our bikes. Now, before we set out, we'd better make sure all our watches say the same. It's exactly twelve minutes past two now, and Django has promised to turn up at all those places at exactly three o'clock. So we'd better hurry. Remember, in his letter he told us not to speak to him when we saw him – he'd speak first if he felt like it! Right – we meet back at the garden shed at four to compare notes.'

The children all set off. Janet and Colin didn't have far to go – the Dog and Duck inn was only ten minutes' walk along the main street of the village, and they were soon there. Barbara and George would have to walk more briskly. Spinney Wood was fairly close, but there were twisty pathways leading uphill before they got there, and they wanted to arrive in good time.

Peter, Pam and Jack fetched their bicycles. They had quite a journey ahead of them. They could cycle part of the way to Torling Castle, but then the road went uphill, and it was too steep for bicycles. It didn't go all the way to the castle, either, and they would have to leave their bikes by a stile and go the last part of the way along a footpath.

None of them wanted to be late for the exciting moment when the young magician had promised to appear in three places at once!

By the time Barbara and George, feeling rather breathless, arrived at the big oak tree in Spinney Wood, Janet and Colin had been waiting for almost half an hour outside the Dog and Duck. Nobody had seen any sign of Django. But he must be *somewhere* close!

Just a moment or so before three o'clock, Peter, Pam and Jack arrived outside the ruins of Torling Castle. It had been hard work, cycling uphill and running the rest of the way. They sat down on some rocks and waited. The magic was supposed to happen in less than a minute!

Peter looked at his watch and began a countdown, just as if he expected an interplanetary rocket to take off. 'Twenty-nine, twenty-eight, twenty-seven, twenty-six, twenty-five, twenty-four . . .'

George was doing just the same thing in Spinney Wood. 'Twenty-three, twenty-two, twenty-one, twenty . . .'

And so were Colin and Janet, outside the Dog and Duck. 'Fifteen, fourteen, thirteen, twelve, eleven . . .'

Only a few seconds to go now!

The Seven were all waiting in suspense. The road outside the Dog and Duck was as quiet as usual at this time of day. There wasn't a breath of wind in the trees of Spinney Wood. And only the loud calls of the jackdaws broke the silence at Torling Castle.

'Five, four, three, two, one – zero!' said Peter.

And at that very moment Django appeared in the arched gateway of the old castle!

Crack! There was a rustle of branches in Spinney Wood – and Django jumped down from the big oak tree and landed at the feet of the astonished George and Barbara.

'Hallo!' said a voice from the doorway of the Dog and Duck. 'Here I am!'

And Janet and Colin turned to see Django standing there and smiling at them!

Chapter Six

A PAIR OF RED SOCKS

Less than an hour later the Seven were holding a meeting in the garden shed. They were all completely baffled. Everyone was talking at once, very excitedly, asking questions to which nobody had any answers. The noise was simply deafening!

'Silence!' shouted Peter. 'Now, we'll all take turns to say what happened, or we'll never get anywhere!'

'Well, you see, Django . . .' George and Janet both started together.

'I said one at a time!' Peter told them crossly. 'You start, Janet!'

'Well, Colin and I were standing outside the Dog and Duck when we heard Django say, "Hallo, here I am!" I know it was exactly three o'clock, because Colin was counting the seconds!'

'Was that all he said?' asked Jack.

'Yes, that was all,' said Colin.

'And then what happened?' asked Peter.

'Then he just made a sort of sign, as if he wanted us to stay where we were, and he went off down the road,' said Janet. 'As soon as he was out of sight we came straight here.'

'You're sure you couldn't have made a mistake? It really *was* Django, was it?' asked Peter.

'We're quite sure it was Django,' Janet told him.

'Barbara and George – what about you two?' asked Peter. 'What happened to *you*?'

'We got quite a fright!' said Barbara. 'He simply dropped out of the tree and landed at our feet!'

'He must have been hiding *up* the tree when we arrived, of course,' George pointed out. 'Otherwise we'd have been sure to see and hear him climbing it.'

'Unless he really *did* get there by magic, of course!' laughed Colin.

'Aren't you convinced *yet*, Colin?' said Jack. 'I don't know what more proof you want!'

'I want the last two proofs he's promised!' said Colin at once.

Peter sighed. He wished Colin wouldn't be so nasty and suspicious about their new friend. 'Well, I can assure you,' he said, 'there wasn't anyone up at the castle when we got there, and Django did appear, the very moment he'd said he would. If there's a trick in it, I'd jolly well like to know how it was done! And there's one thing even Colin can't deny: we *did* see Django in three different places at the very same time – three o'clock exactly. We know we weren't asleep, so it can't have been a dream or anything. Django was there in the flesh – the same boy who comes to our school, in his blue boiler suit and blue socks and

45

sneakers, and he even spoke to you and Janet. So what have you got to say about *that*, Colin?'

Colin couldn't think of anything at all to say! There was quite a long silence, and Peter began to feel a little sorry he'd spoken so sharply.

But to everyone's surprise, Barbara did have something to say. 'Blue socks?' she asked. 'You did say *blue* socks, didn't you, Peter?'

'Yes, blue socks – the sort he always wears,' said Peter. 'At least, he's worn blue socks ever since *we* knew him!'

'That's funny, because he was wearing *red* socks when we saw him in Spinney Wood!' said Barbara.

'She's right – they *were* red,' George agreed. 'They were right in front of my nose when Django jumped out of that tree, so I know!'

'What did you two see?' Peter asked Colin and Janet. 'Did you notice what colour socks he was wearing?'

'No, I'm afraid not,' said Janet.

'I'm sure they were blue,' said Colin.

'Well, that really is odd!' Peter sounded surprised. 'If we all saw Django at once, why was one of him, and only one, wearing red socks? Supposing it was a kind of magic reflection of him we saw – well, if I'm wearing blue socks and I look at myself in the mirror, *my* reflection isn't wearing red socks. So that means . . .'

'That means you're coming round to my way of thinking!' Colin told him. 'You suspect it's all a hoax.

You can see Django must be an impostor.'

'Oh no, he isn't!' Barbara interrupted. 'Have you forgotten all the other things he's done, Colin? Could *you* have stopped the Big Wheel at the fair, or got Scamper to do arithmetic, or turned up in three places at once, come to that? I mean, the colour of his socks doesn't make any difference to the amazing things he's shown us he can do.'

'Barbara is right!' said Pam loyally. She just couldn't imagine how Django could be an impostor.

'What about that candy floss woman at the fair, though?' said Colin. 'He seemed to know her very well, and I'm not sure I believe his explanation. And there's the way Scamper spent ages sniffing around that "flying trunk" of his the other day, growling at it as if there was something wrong with it. Dogs have very good instincts. And now we have this mystery of the red and blue socks. I call it all very suspicious!'

'But you can't put your finger on anything for certain, can you?' asked Jack.

'No, not exactly,' Colin admitted. 'All the same, you must admit there's something fishy going on!'

'Let's ask him about it at school on Monday,' Peter suggested. 'I'm sure he'll tell us the truth.'

'Woof! Woof!' barked Scamper — just as if *he* wanted to know the truth too. Perhaps he hadn't thought the Land of Magic was a very nice place after all!

On Monday morning Peter and Jack were early for

school. The school gates weren't open yet, so they had to wait in the road outside.

'Look, there he is!' said Jack, pointing to the corner of the road.

Sure enough, Django had just appeared at the crossroads, and was walking towards them, whistling a tune which the two boys seemed to know. After a moment they recognised it: it was a tune that had been played as part of the fairground music, so everybody in the village knew it. Now they came to think of it, Django had been whistling it last week too – he seemed to have it on the brain!

'Hallo, Django,' said Peter, as Django came up to them. 'Did you have a nice weekend?'

'Very nice, thank you!' said the young magician, smiling.

'I say – what you showed us on Saturday really *was* amazing! And now we'd like you to explain it,' said Peter.

'Oh – I can't do that!' said Django. 'That's my magic secret.'

'You could at least tell us which of the three Djangos we saw was *really* you,' said Jack.

'Well, all right! I was the one at the Dog and Duck.'

'What about the other two?' asked Peter, feeling very interested.

'Those were just imaginary. I wasn't really in Spinney Wood or at Torling Castle. I just *projected* a mental picture of myself there.'

'That really is amazing!' said Jack.

'Then why was one of the imaginary Djangos not the same as the real one?' asked Peter.

'What do you mean?' said Django. All of a sudden he sounded cross. 'He *was*! He must have been!'

'Actually, Peter's right!' said Jack. 'You were wearing blue socks outside the Dog and Duck and at Torling Castle, but *red* socks in Spinney Wood!'

Django opened his mouth as if to say something, but no words came out.

'Well, can you explain that?' asked Peter.

'Er – yes, yes, I can! It's perfectly simple!' stammered Django. 'You remember I told you I was still learning? Well, it's the same as the first colour televisions, when they hadn't got it quite right yet. Sometimes you saw newsreaders with green hair and pink eyes and so on! It's a bit like that with me. The mental pictures I project aren't absolutely perfect yet down to every single detail.'

'But of course they *will* be, once you've practised?' said Peter. He sounded slightly disbelieving.

Just then the school gates were opened, and the boys waiting outside were allowed into the playground. Django hurried off, telling Peter and Jack he had to go and find a pair of shorts he'd left in the gym changing room.

'He seemed a bit flustered, didn't he?' said Jack, as Django walked away.

'Yes – and I thought his explanation was rather peculiar!' said Peter. 'You know, I'm beginning to suspect Colin may have been right all along.'

'We must be fair to Django, though,' said Jack. 'Let's wait and see what his last two proofs are; and then, if we think he's trying to trick us, we'll confront him!'

Chapter Seven

A SPRINTING RECORD!

At break, Jack and Peter asked Django when he was going to give them the last two proofs of his magic powers that Colin wanted.

Django thought for a moment. Then he said, 'I'll give you the sixth proof on Wednesday – that's the day after tomorrow. It will be after school, on the outskirts of the village, where they've built those new houses.'

So after school on Wednesday, the Seven all gathered at the crossroads near the place where a lot of houses had recently been built.

When Django joined them, he seemed to have all his confidence back again. His green eyes were sparkling. Pam, Barbara and Janet thought he was more fascinating than ever.

'I want you all to stand here on the pavement,' Django told the children. 'I'm going to draw a magic circle round you with this piece of chalk – and whatever happens you mustn't step outside the circle, or the magic won't work!'

As he spoke, he was drawing a circle on the pavement in red chalk.

'There!' said Django, when he had finished drawing the circle. 'Now I'll tell you about the amazing sight you're about to see! You see that block of houses over there?' Django went on. He pointed to a big block of new houses on the other side of the road. 'It's fifty metres square – I measured it this morning. Well, I bet you I can run round it in less than twenty seconds. And I can do that three times without stopping, too!'

'You mean you can run two hundred metres in less than twenty seconds?' said George in amazement. He liked mental arithmetic, and it hadn't taken him a moment to work out the distance Django would have to run along all four sides of the block.

'That's right!' said Django. 'Yes – you'll be able to see me go faster than the world's greatest Olympic sprinters!'

Pam, Janet and Barbara were full of admiration. George was thoroughly puzzled! As for Peter, Jack and Colin – well, the disbelieving smiles on their faces said louder than any words that they thought it was too good to be true.

Without wasting any more time, Django got down on a starting-line at the corner of the block of houses.

Peter got out his stopwatch and began counting. 'Five, four, three, two, one . . .'

'Go!' shouted Barbara, at the top of her voice.

And Django went! He shot off in such a hurry that

he nearly knocked down a lady who was walking along the road carrying a big shopping basket, but luckily he managed to swerve aside just before colliding with her.

'Oh dear, he'll never do it if people keep getting in his way!' said Pam. She sounded worried.

'Who knows, maybe it's an obstacle race?' said Peter, rather sarcastically.

'Or a slalom, like in ski-ing!' said Jack.

'Or a gymkhana with jumps and so on!' laughed Colin.

The three girls couldn't understand the boys' attitude. They didn't see anything funny themselves.

Django was still going very fast. Soon he would turn the next corner of the block.

'He's out of sight!' said Janet.

'How many seconds since he started?' asked Pam excitedly.

'Nine,' said Peter, looking at the stopwatch.

'Then he's going to lose his bet,' said Colin. 'If he had any chance of winning it, he'd have had to . . .'

But whatever he was going to say, he didn't say it, because Barbara interrupted him.

'Look! Here he comes again!' she cried.

They all turned their heads — and saw Django coming into sight round the other corner of the block! He was racing towards them. He didn't slow down at all as he got close.

'Golly, that's amazing!' said Janet. 'He *is* going to do it in under twenty seconds!'

'He'll never manage it three times without stopping, though,' said Colin. 'Not at that speed! He'll run out of breath!'

'Nineteen seconds!' announced Peter, as Django passed, giving them a wave. The children couldn't see why Scamper yapped at him angrily several times. Perhaps the spaniel had misunderstood Django's friendly gesture?

Next moment, Django had disappeared round the corner of the block again.

'Twenty-seven seconds, twenty-eight, twenty-nine.' Peter was counting the seconds out loud.

'Here he comes!' cried George.

'What, already?' exclaimed Colin in astonishment.

'But that's impossible!' whispered the surprised Peter. However, Django *was* racing full tilt towards them again. He was about to finish his second run round the block of houses.

'Thirty-seven seconds!' announced Peter in a loud voice.

Looking very pleased, Django flashed them a wide smile in passing.

'I say – that's *not* Django!' Jack breathed.

'Woof! Woof!' barked Scamper.

'No – it's not!' agreed Colin.

The others stared at them in surprise. Meanwhile, the running boy went off down the road again as fast as he could go, and disappeared round the corner once more.

'Whatever makes you say such a nasty thing?' Pam asked Jack and Colin angrily.

'Ssh!' hissed Jack. 'He's coming back!'

Yes – Django was running back towards them, with a big smile on his face. He was going to win his bet!

He stopped right in front of the Seven.

'Fifty-six seconds!' said Peter, looking at his stopwatch.

'Jolly well done, Django!' cried the three girls. 'You were terrific!'

The young magician wasn't even out of breath! He was grinning happily, and his bright eyes and white teeth showed up in his tanned face. Obviously he was delighted to hear the girls praise him.

In a moment or so, however, he realised that the boys weren't as enthusiastic as Janet, Pam and Barbara. None of *them* had congratulated him on his amazing run! And Scamper kept sniffing at him, as if there was something wrong . . .

'Er – Django,' said George. 'You'd only just disappeared round one corner of the block when you came into sight again round the other. So it only took you two or three seconds to run round the two sides of the block we couldn't see – but it took you almost twenty to run along the two sides we *could* see! That's a bit odd, isn't it?'

'It's magic!' Django told him. 'You wouldn't understand!'

'We're not such idiots as you seem to think!' said Colin angrily. 'I think we could understand perfectly well if you'd condescend to explain!'

Peter wished Colin didn't sound so cross. He couldn't see any point in offending Django. It would be better to coax the truth out of him. Peter had found out by now that his new friend had a weakness for compliments – so why not take advantage of that?

'I think you must have broken the world sprinting record!' he said. 'In fact, I'm *sure* you did! But don't you see – we won't be able to appreciate your amazing performance properly unless you can explain it. I don't want you to tell us all your secrets, of course. Just give us a little hint. I bet your knowledge of magic will really amaze us if we can get some idea of it!'

Jack and Colin winked at each other. *They* saw what Peter's plan was. Unfortunately, it didn't work as well as he had hoped.

'I can't really tell you any more than you know already,' said Django. 'It's the same as when I appeared in three places at once. You *thought* you were seeing me – but really it was only the mental picture of me I was projecting!'

'Oh, *didn't* you run round the block three times?' asked Janet, quite upset.

Django smiled. 'Well, no! I couldn't really run six hundred metres in under a minute,' he admitted. 'I only ran round the block once. But as soon as I was out of sight of you, I sent my image whizzing round the block twice, while I trotted round at a comfortable pace myself. So you saw my image pass you twice – but I only had to do one round, and come back to the finishing-line feeling fresh as a daisy!'

'Goodness gracious!' said Pam, shaking her head. 'I don't think I *quite* understand, Django. It's even worse than those maths questions we get at school, about taps dripping at different speeds.'

'Don't worry, Pam, I can explain it to you!' Colin told her.

'Yes, that's all right, we can explain it!' Jack agreed.

The two boys couldn't wait to be on their own with the rest of the Seven, and tell them what they had found out about Django.

Chapter Eight

THE MYSTERY OF THE MISSING TOOTH

Once they had said goodbye to Django, the Seven went to the garden shed and locked the door behind them. Now they could talk secrets and no one would overhear them.

Peter hadn't seen what Jack and Colin had seen, because he was glancing at his stopwatch every time Django passed them. He asked what they all wanted to know.

'What makes you two so sure it wasn't Django?' he said to Jack and Colin.

'His tooth!' they replied at the very same moment.

'His *tooth*?' asked Barbara in surprise.

'That's right – his tooth. Or rather, *not* his tooth, if you see what I mean!' said Jack mysteriously. Except for Colin, the others didn't see what he meant at all. 'Listen – didn't any of the rest of you notice? The second time he came round and smiled at us, he had a tooth missing!'

'And Django certainly hasn't got a tooth missing,' said Colin. 'We all know that.'

'I say, you're right! Now I come to think of it, there

was a kind of dark hole on one side of his mouth,' said George. 'But he went by so fast I hardly noticed.'

'Oh dear!' said Janet. 'I think *I* saw that, too. But I didn't work out what it was.'

'So he had a tooth missing – what do we deduce from that?' asked Peter thoughtfully.

'It wasn't Django at all, that's what we deduce!' said Colin. 'And if it wasn't Django, it stands to reason it was somebody else.'

'But that's impossible!' cried Pam. 'They were as like as two peas in a pod.'

'Yes, and that's only to be expected,' said Barbara. 'Django explained it, didn't he? About mental images being – being projected, and so on.'

'I'm afraid that's sheer nonsense,' said Colin. 'You remember what Django told us about illusionism or pure magic? And he gave us that example – about a window opening on a beautiful countryside. If the illusionist is clever enough, he makes the person listening to him think he actually does see what the illusionist is describing – but really, the picture is going to come out of that person's own memory. It'll be a picture of something or somebody familiar that the illusionist conjures up. And that means it *can't* be any different from the thing his hearers are remembering – it depends on their own memories! So this pure magic of Django's is a matter of getting people into a frame of mind where they think what they remember is actually something *real*! Do you see what I mean?'

'Well – I *think* so!' said Janet doubtfully, although Colin's train of thought was really rather beyond her.

'All right, then! So it would be quite impossible for us to think we saw something we'd never seen before – something that couldn't come out of our memories. Like Django with one tooth missing!'

'I say – that's awfully clever, Colin,' Peter admitted. 'Jolly good thinking! You've convinced *me* all right.'

'Me too,' said George.

'And me!' said Barbara and Janet in chorus, very sadly.

Pam was the only one who didn't say anything. Poor Pam! She couldn't bear to admit that Django had been tricking them, even if she did see that Colin's explanation was probably right.

'But then who *was* the Django with a missing tooth?' asked Barbara. She was baffled.

So were the others! 'Perhaps he's got a brother?' suggested Peter, though he didn't sound very sure of himself.

'That's possible,' said Colin. 'But remember, Django himself confessed to running only the beginning and end parts of the race round the block – and there were *three* rounds. That means he must have a second accomplice.'

'Yes, of course!' said Pam, suddenly remembering something which convinced even *her*. 'When he appeared to us at the same time in three different places – Torling Castle, Spinney Wood and the Dog and Duck – the same two accomplices must have been helping him to play that trick too!'

'Wait a minute – aren't we being a bit over-imaginative?' asked George. 'One other person who looks just like Django seems quite hard to believe in, but *two* other people . . . well, that really does take some swallowing!'

'I tell you what!' said Peter. 'Django still has to give us one more proof of his magic powers. We'll

make sure that that's our chance to find out the truth.'

'Yes – why don't we ask him to appear three times at the same moment *and* in the same place?' said Colin. 'And when we've got all three Djangos there in front of us . . .'

'We'll jump on them!' said Jack.

'Woof! Woof!' barked Scamper. It sounded as if he thought that would be a good idea and wanted to join in too!

'Calm down, everyone,' said Peter. 'We don't want to hurt anyone – that wouldn't be like the Secret Seven at all. No, I've got a better idea. It will be much more fun, too!'

He paused for a moment, to make sure everybody was listening. Then he went on in a low voice.

'We'll use that super cine-camera Jack's Uncle Bob gave us. If our friend Django really *is* the great illusionist he claims to be, all we'll see on the screen when we show our film is *one* Django. A camera hasn't got any imagination or memory, you see – it only photographs what's really and truly there. But if there are *three* Djangos on the film, it means the Django we know has been hoaxing us! And then we'll decide what to do about it – but not before then!'

'Yes,' said Jack. 'I call that a very good idea, Peter!'

The others all agreed. The only question was, how could they find a good time and a good excuse for carrying out their plan?

And then Peter had another brilliant idea! They would suggest a performance by Django at the end-of-term school concert – and ask him to give them his seventh proof at the same time. It would be the perfect moment!

Chapter Nine

THE SCHOOL CONCERT

There was always a big concert and entertainment at the end of the summer term. The boys' school and the girls' school both took part in it, and even some of the nursery school children too! There were too many people in the audience for the concert to be held in one of the school halls, and so a big open-air stage was set up on wooden trestles on the playing-field of the boys' school.

It was going to be a very interesting concert this year. Peter and Jack had told Django what the Seven wanted him to do, and although at first he didn't seem very keen on the idea of giving his seventh proof in front of such a huge audience, all the rest of their class wanted to see him do his magic tricks! So in the end he had to take up the Secret Seven's challenge.

On the day of the concert there was a huge crowd in the school grounds. Luckily it was a very fine day. Classes from all the village schools took part in the show. Some did folk dances, some sang songs, and some of them gave exhibitions of gymnastics. There were loudspeakers to announce each number as it was about to begin.

Pam, Barbara and Janet had volunteered to sell programmes. That meant they'd have seats kept for them not too far from the stage – an important part of their plan!

All the children's parents sat watching the show, in rows and rows of seats raised in tiers on wooden platforms like seats in a theatre, so that everyone could get a good view. The audience were clapping all the turns enthusiastically.

George and Colin's class gave a very successful gymnastics display. They ended up with a 'human pyramid'. Five rows of boys formed up, standing on each other's shoulders. Colin, who was thin and didn't weigh an awful lot, was at the very top, standing on the shoulders of George and one other boy. He stood there and unfurled a flag in the school colours – and then the pyramid came apart again, the boys jumped down on the stage, and bowed to the audience.

But what all the Secret Seven were really waiting for was Django's show!

There was an interval in the concert just before his turn came. During the interval there were all sorts of comings and goings on the stage. Boys from Jack and Peter's class kept carrying up strange objects, and the audience were getting interested even before the show began.

A large, shiny black trunk was placed in the middle

of the stage, and the boys unrolled a big black backcloth and hung it from posts at the back of the platform. There were silver stars on the backcloth – and a pair of huge green eyes like Django's, painted in phosphorescent paint!

Mysterious music began to play while the boys finished setting the scene and the audience went back to their seats for the second half of the concert. When the spectators were all in place, and sitting quietly, the music stopped. There was complete silence.

Peter climbed up on the stage with a microphone in his hand.

'Ladies and gentlemen, parents and teachers!' he announced. 'You are about to see an amazing, unique performance! Nothing like it can be seen anywhere else in the world! The extraordinary magician who will appear before you is descended from a long line of enchanters! He has astonishing powers which will hold you spellbound! But it's time I let his magic speak for itself! Allow me to introduce the one and only amazing – DJANGO!'

And Peter jumped down again.

'Jolly good!' Colin whispered to him.

There was a deafening clash of cymbals, the shiny black trunk on the stage opened – and out stepped Django!

Didn't he look fine! Just for once, he wasn't wearing his boiler suit. He had changed in the school cloakroom, and now he was in a gorgeous Eastern costume. His dark hair was hidden by a white turban with a stone that looked like an emerald in it, the same colour as his eyes. He had a long, almond-green silk coat embroidered with gold and sequins, and a smart lilac waistcoat underneath it. His white linen trousers were held up by a gold belt, and he wore beautiful leather slippers on his feet.

Django walked to the front of the stage and bowed to his audience. Behind the scenes, the boys in charge of music turned on the tape-recorder, and Oriental music came over the loudspeakers.

There wasn't a sound from the audience – Django seemed to have them spellbound already! He took hold of the microphone.

'Ladies and gentlemen,' he said, in a deep and mysterious voice, 'you are about to witness some very unusual things! It is my duty to warn you that anyone who has a very nervous disposition might be scared . . .'

'I say, he's really piling it on thick today!' Colin whispered. He and Peter were standing to one side at the foot of the stage.

'Yes – he sounds so sure of himself, maybe he'll conjure up *nine* Djangos instead of just three!' said Peter, smiling.

Django, up on the stage, had noticed the two of them talking, and just for a moment he hesitated. Then he went on with his speech of introduction. It was the sort of patter the Seven had heard from him before, so Peter and Colin didn't listen very hard. Jack and George came up and joined them.

'Gosh, that trunk weighed a tonne!' Jack whispered to the others. 'I bet the other two Djangos are inside it.'

'Why don't we open it and see?' said George.

'No, that wouldn't be fair!' Peter told him. 'Anyway, we'd be spoiling the show for everyone else – and the Head would be simply furious with us!'

'Look at the girls,' Jack said. 'They're signalling to us!'

Now that half the concert was over, Pam, Janet and Barbara didn't have to sell any more programmes. They were sitting in the audience, two rows from the front, with a big cardboard box on their knees. The box had a hole cut in one side of it.

'It's all right – the boys have seen us!' said Janet. 'We'll start filming when they give us the sign.'

'Is everything ready?' asked Pam.

'Yes,' said Barbara. But she checked once more. Everything was as it ought to be: the camera was well hidden inside the box, and only its lens stuck out a little way through the hole cut in the side.

Django was going on with his patter.

'You must not confuse conjuring tricks or sleight-of-hand with illusionism, or pure magic. When a magician practises sleight-of-hand, he is diverting the audience's attention from what is really going on . . .'

He took a shiny coin out of one of his pockets, tossed it in the air and caught it again, juggling with it so nimbly that in the end the audience couldn't tell just where it was! Then he asked a little boy sitting in the front row to come up on stage, and he plucked the coin out of thin air at the end of the little boy's nose – just the same trick as he had played on Pam!

The crowd were surprised and pleased, and applauded Django. Even the Head, who was supposed to be a very strict man, was smiling and clapping!

Django looked pleased with himself and bowed to the audience several times.

The four boys were beginning to get impatient. 'Here we go again!' muttered Colin. 'His performance doesn't change much, does it? I bet you anything we get the open window next, and the blue sky and church bells and so on!'

Sure enough, at that very moment Django was saying, 'Now, if I could make an open window seem to appear on that backcloth, with blue sky and green meadows and fields of golden corn beyond it, and if I could make you think you heard church bells ringing in the distance and you saw a bird come to perch on the window-sill, singing a lovely song . . .'

Django was making dramatic gestures as he went through his patter. He crossed the stage with one hand to his ear, as if he were listening to the bells, and then went to the other side of the stage to 'listen' to the song of the bird! All the time, the music was playing softly.

'You know, he's getting better at it,' Jack said. 'Maybe he *will* conjure up that open window one day!'

'Keep an eye on that trunk!' George whispered. 'I'm sure I saw it move a moment ago.'

'Django's getting at you – him and his talk about illusions,' said Colin. 'It's much too heavy to move on its own. Jack said it weighed a tonne!'

'Ssh!' whispered Peter. 'The big moment's coming!'

'What you are about to see is not myself, but a mental picture of me,' Django was telling the audience. 'If the spirits are favourable, you will see not one but *two* mental pictures of me, following me about and doing exactly what I do, like living shadows!'

He went over to the trunk.

'Now he opens it and the other two come out, I bet!' said George.

'And to avoid any misunderstanding,' Django went on, 'let me show you that this trunk is completely empty!'

He opened it – and everyone could see there was nothing at all inside.

'Gosh – I'd have lost my bet!' said George. He was really startled.

'Yes, we weren't expecting that,' Jack admitted.

'But where *are* the other two, I wonder?' said Colin, frowning.

Peter was about to say something when Django took a little glass bottle out of his pocket and shook its contents out on the stage. At once, thick white vapour rose from the boards! Peter was only just in time to signal to the girls that they were to start the cine-camera filming – then the thick, artificial mists hid him from their eyes.

The surprised audience were loving every moment of the show! They were murmuring their approval. Several people had got to their feet, to try and get a better view of what was going on. Barbara, Pam and Janet were afraid the man sitting in the row in front of them might get up too, and hide the stage from the camera lens. But luckily he didn't move!

Django, up on the stage, was dancing in time to the music now. He wove his way in and out of the mists – and then he disappeared entirely for a moment. When he came out of the mist again, he was being followed by his double: a boy in a beautiful Eastern costume just like his own!

The double followed Django and copied every move he made. It was like watching a living, breathing shadow of the magician.

'He really *is* clever!' exclaimed Pam. 'Honestly, what does it matter if it's real magic or not? It's so pretty to watch!'

Barbara and Janet, sitting beside her, were enjoying the performance too, drinking in every moment of it. And so was the camera on their knees – humming quietly away inside its cardboard box!

Django disappeared into the mists again – and came out followed by *two* doubles! There were gasps of amazement from the audience. The two doubles imitated every movement he made, at almost exactly the same time. The three boys in their Eastern costumes danced together for a few moments, moving mysteriously in and out of the mists. The vapour had spread out over the whole of the back part of the stage now, but the front of the stage was clear. The three Djangos came forward and stood quite still in front of the audience.

And what a surprise the spectators had when they spoke! All three mouths moved, forming the words – but the *sound* of a human voice came from only one of them. Django's two doubles made no sound at all.

'Ladies and gentlemen!' said Django. 'You see before you what appear to be three identical people –

but as I told you earlier, two are just illusions, and only one is really flesh and blood!'

Hidden in its box, the cine-camera was still filming! It didn't know or care about illusions! But the three girls were spellbound – they had quite forgotten their suspicions of Django. His performance was certainly a great success, however he had worked his magic tricks!

Jack, Peter, Colin and George, however, were beginning to get impatient. They couldn't see as much of Django's performance from where they were standing as the girls could, up in their seats among the audience. The boys could only hear Django's patter, and they knew that off by heart – after all, he had been at school in the village for nearly a month now.

'And now,' Django was saying, mysteriously, 'I will send these two images of myself back to the land of dreams! They will dissolve into the mist and turn to nothing again!'

Slowly and solemnly, he walked backwards into the mist. So did his two doubles.

As the applause began, Django stepped forward again and came out into daylight at the front of the stage – but now he was all by himself!

Chapter Ten

AFTER THE SHOW

The audience clapped and cheered till they were hoarse! Even Susie and Binkie, who had said they were sure nobody who was friends with the Seven could put on a show worth watching, were clapping hard! So was the Headmaster, Mr Kirby, and *he* didn't often get carried away by enthusiasm.

Django bowed low for the last time, stepped back, and disappeared into the mist again.

But the applause went on and on. The audience wanted him to come back. 'Django! Django! Django!' they shouted.

However, there was no sign of Django. The mists began to drift away, and the whole stage came into sight again. You could see Django's green eyes painted on the backcloth. They looked as if they were emerging from a sea of clouds.

'Django! Django! Django!' people went on shouting.

But still Django didn't come back – and the boys

soon realised why. This time there was absolutely no deception at all! Django really *had* disappeared.

'He's run for it!' said Peter. 'He knows we'll be after him! Quick – we must try and find him!'

And the four boys started searching at once. First they explored the underneath of the stage. There was a whole forest of trestles holding the boards up above ground level, and they thought he might be hiding in there. Jack and Colin went down on all fours and crawled right in. But they didn't find Django.

'If he really has run away from us, that means he has a guilty conscience!' said Colin.

'There are four ways out of the school grounds,' said Peter. 'Let's each go and watch one of them. We'll meet back at the main entrance after everyone's gone home.'

The four of them separated and went off, one to each of the gates leading out of the grounds.

At last the audience realised that Django wasn't coming back. They stopped shouting for him, and the applause died down.

Pam, Barbara and Janet felt that something had gone wrong, but they didn't know what. They had seen the boys searching underneath the stage, and then running off. But sitting where they were, right in the middle of the audience, they couldn't go to join them without disturbing a lot of other people. The rows of seats were very close together.

'Oh dear – we're stuck here till the end of the

concert!' whispered Pam crossly.

'Where've they gone?' asked Janet.

'To look for Django, I suppose,' said Barbara.

They had to sit through some singing by one of the school choirs, and a little play performed by the nursery school children, and then at last the concert came to an end.

The audience clapped everyone for their hard work, and after the Headmaster had made his closing speech, they began to leave their seats and make for the exits from the school grounds.

The four boys stayed at their posts for what seemed like ages. At last almost everybody had left – and they hadn't seen Django among the crowd anywhere!

They went to the main entrance, where they found Pam, Barbara and Janet waiting for them.

'What's happened?' the girls all asked eagerly. 'Do tell us!'

'Django's run away!' Peter told them. 'He took advantage of the artificial mist he was using as part of his show – it helped him to get away from us without being seen.'

'I'm sure he'd guessed we were suspicious of him,' said Colin. 'Otherwise he'd have been only too pleased to wait for us – he'd be looking forward to our congratulations. He simply loves praise and compliments!'

'There's no need to be so nasty about it, Colin!' Pam snapped. 'You disliked Django from the very start, didn't you? I can't think why – he's never done you any harm! What's wrong with liking praise if you can do something to deserve it? And he's done all sorts of things to entertain us!'

'*And* to make fools of us, too!' said Colin. He wasn't going to let Pam get round him.

'Well, *you* just try doing some of those tricks of his!' said Pam crossly. 'You're very good at talking, but that's all!'

Several of the last people leaving the grounds turned round at the noise of this quarrel, to see what was going on.

'That's quite enough of that!' said Peter firmly. 'The show's over now – there's no need to put on another performance! You can settle your differences somewhere else. Let's go home now.'

The Seven started out. They left the school grounds, and walked down the road.

'Did you girls manage to film Django's show?' asked Jack.

'Yes, that's all right!' said Barbara, tapping the cardboard box. She was carrying it under her arm. 'Now we must send the film away to be developed. I do hope everything comes out!'

'It's usually five days before we get a film back,' grumbled George. 'Five whole days before we'll know for certain what it shows! What a nuisance!'

'Oh, five days will soon pass!' said Peter. 'Don't forget, the summer holidays have just begun. And we haven't found Django yet, either. I've got an idea that looking for him may take quite a long time!'

Chapter Eleven

THE CINE-FILM

Peter was quite right.

The Seven spent the first two days of the holidays looking all over the village, but they couldn't find Django anywhere.

'I say – his father is working on the site where they're building the new main road, isn't he?' Barbara suddenly remembered. 'Why don't we go and look for Mr Papiropesco? *He'll* be able to tell us where Django is!'

'Good idea, Barbara!' said Peter approvingly. 'Let's get our bikes out and go to look for him at once.'

Ten minutes later, the Seven were cycling towards the place where the new main road was being built. They took a short cut along a woodland pathway. Their bicycles didn't make any sound on the soft moss. A squirrel shot away as they rode past. The girls would have liked to stop and pick wild strawberries – they saw a lot of them growing in a sunny clearing. But they were all so anxious to find out about Django that they didn't stop.

As they came to the edge of the wood they heard the sound of machinery working. They must be getting close to the building site.

Not far away, they saw a place where what had once been part of a field was all churned up. There were men mixing cement, and bulldozers at work, making a lot of noise.

The Seven left their bicycles at the edge of the wood and walked up to the men building the road. They went up to the man who was nearest to them.

'Good morning,' Peter said. 'We're looking for Mr Papiropesco. Could you tell us which one he is?'

The man was puzzled. 'What was the name you said again?'

'Mr Papiropesco.'

'Funny sort of name! I don't know anyone like that here,' said the man. 'Still, you could ask the foreman. Look, that's him! Over there on top of that mound of earth.'

'Thank you very much,' said Peter politely. And he walked on, with the rest of the Seven following him.

'Odd!' Colin was muttering. 'Very odd indeed!'

They went up to the mound of earth. The foreman was standing on top of it, and they didn't speak to him at once, because they could see he was busy directing a very tricky operation. There was a huge bucket of freshly mixed cement hanging from the arm of a crane, and it had to be poured into a deep hole. The foreman was holding what looked like a little box – it was a device which meant he could manoeuvre

81

the arm of the crane by remote control. The children watched with great interest as he successfully finished the job.

'Hallo, children!' said the foreman, who had noticed them watching him. 'There, you've just seen us laying the foundations of a big new road intersection! And what can I do for *you*?' He gave them a friendly smile.

'We're looking for Mr Papiropesco,' Peter said. 'He works here – could you tell us where to find him?'

'Papiropesco, did you say? I'm afraid there's no one of that name working here. There must be some mistake.'

'Oh, but his own son told us he was working on the building of the new main road!' Pam said firmly.

'Well, this is certainly going to be the new main road,' said the foreman, 'but as I've told you, there's nobody called Papiropesco working on it. I'd know if there was – it's not the kind of name you'd forget in a hurry, is it? I'm very sorry.'

'Oh dear, so are we!' said Peter, feeling baffled. 'Well, I'm sorry we bothered you, sir. Goodbye.'

They turned away, feeling puzzled and downcast. So Django *had* been lying to them, even about this. His father wasn't working on the new road at all.

'He's been fooling us all along!' said Colin angrily. 'His father isn't working on the new main road, any more than Django himself can work magic! He's just a cheat and a liar!'

Pam dared not say anything. It was only too clear

that Django *had* been lying, and yet she did like him so much. He was so good-looking, and such fun too. But she could tell Colin wouldn't think much of that as an argument in his favour.

'Colin's right,' Jack agreed. 'We've been hoaxed. We must find Django and teach him a jolly good lesson!'

'Yes,' said Peter. 'But *where* are we going to find him?'

That was quite a difficult question! The Seven were trying to work out an answer all the way home – and this time they stopped in the wood to enjoy the delicious wild strawberries!

A couple of days later, Peter sent notes round to all the Secret Seven, summoning them to an emergency meeting. The new password was 'wild strawberries'.

Pam came running along to the garden shed, late as usual and out of breath. 'Wild strawberries!' she gasped.

Peter opened the door and let her in.

'Sorry I'm late!' she panted.

'It's all right,' said Peter. 'Just for once, you're not the last! George isn't here yet.'

'Oh, you've got the film back!' exclaimed Pam, seeing that Peter and Janet had set up the projector. There was a white sheet hung over one wall of the shed for a screen, and a new reel of film lying on the table.

'Yes, it came this morning,' Janet told her. 'They

only took *four* days to develop it instead of the usual five. Wasn't that lucky?'

'Has it come out all right?'

'Nobody's seen it yet,' said Colin. 'We didn't think it was fair to run the film until *everyone* was here – even the late people!'

Pam didn't answer back. She knew she deserved what he said – she simply couldn't manage to be punctual. But where was George?

'George usually arrives on time!' said Jack, sounding quite worried.

'Oh, I do hope he isn't ill or anything,' said Janet. 'He'll be so disappointed if he doesn't see the film with the rest of us.'

At that moment there was a knock on the door.

'Password?' asked Peter.

'Wild strawberries!' said George's voice.

Peter opened the door.

'Sorry, everyone,' said George, coming into the shed. 'But I've spent the last ten minutes trying to shake Susie and Binkie off. They were sticking to me like leeches!'

'Oh, those two little pests!' said Jack angrily. 'Well, Susie will be sorry for that when I see her at home this evening!'

Poor Jack! He always felt responsible for the annoying way his sister and her friend acted, although of course the rest of the Seven knew it wasn't *his* fault. Susie and Binkie were just a sort of natural hazard – like a shower of rain or a sudden frost – and there wasn't anything to be done about it.

'Did they see you coming here?' asked Peter.

'No, I managed to shake them off in the High Street,' said George. 'But I bet they guessed I was on my way to the shed.'

'Well, at least they don't know the password,' Jack pointed out, so the others stopped worrying.

Now they couldn't wait to see the film! Barbara pulled a black curtain across the window to shut out the daylight, and the projector began to run.

At first the children couldn't see anything at all on the screen – only a lot of drifting whiteness.

'It hasn't come out!' wailed Pam. 'Oh dear – and the cine-camera would have been really *useful* in helping us solve the mystery of Django!'

'It looks like clouds,' said Jack.

'I know what it is. It's the sky!' cried Barbara. 'We must have had the lens pointing the wrong way, and the camera was filming the sky.'

'Oh dear, and we thought we'd been so careful to do everything right!' said Janet. 'Now we've got a boring old film of nothing but clouds!'

'No, wait! It's all right!' cried Peter excitedly. 'Here comes Django! Well done, girls – you did it after all!'

Sure enough, they could see Django appearing on the screen. What they had thought was the sky was really that thick, white, artificial mist. The young magician was dancing gracefully and weaving his way in and out of the white vapour.

'Isn't he good?' sighed Pam. 'All we need is the background music!'

The three girls couldn't help admiring Django's skill! And at last the boys got a proper view of the performance. They hadn't been able to see it at the concert, because the mist hid it from them where they were standing.

In his fine Eastern costume, Django was dancing and swaying about, and making mysterious magic gestures!

'Yes, he *is* quite impressive,' Peter admitted.

'He's a cheat and a liar!' Colin said firmly. *He* wasn't impressed.

'Oh, shut up!' said Pam crossly, and the other girls were darting angry glances at him too. So for once Colin did shut up and let them enjoy the show.

After a while, Django disappeared into the mist again.

'Now for the important part. He's coming back any moment!' said Jack.

'And if there are two people on the film, he was lying to us,' Colin reminded them all. 'If not . . .'

'If not, then he *is* a great magician!' said Pam.

Django would soon reappear! One more second, and the Seven would know the truth. That second seemed to last for ages!

At last, Django came out of the mist . . .

'There *are* two of them!' shouted Colin. 'See? I was right from the start!'

'Yes, he really took us in with his tall tales about magic, didn't he?' said Jack angrily.

'Oh dear, I suppose we ought to have guessed!' said Barbara. 'But I did so want to believe in his magic powers!'

The film was still running. Django went back into the mists again, followed by his double . . . and when he came out, there were three of him!

87

Chapter Twelve

SUSIE IS A HELP!

'That finally proves it!' said Colin. 'Proves it three times over!'

Pam stared sadly at the screen. She wished so much that she could only see one Django there – but she couldn't deny the evidence of her own eyes! She was seeing three Djangos! It was hard for her to accept the facts. She felt sure Django couldn't really be as bad as Colin made out. He was so nice. And if he seemed just a little boastful at times – well, mightn't that be because he really felt shy, and was trying to hide it?

The film came to an end. 'Now we'll run it through again, and watch it in detail,' said Peter.

No one spoke as Barbara rewound the film and fitted it back into the projector. The Seven were all feeling rather upset, in their different ways.

As they watched the film for the second time, they slowed it down to look at the important details. When they did that, they could see that the three Djangos didn't always move at *exactly* the same moment. The third was often a split second behind the other two.

And when the three of them all smiled, the children could easily see that the second Django had a missing tooth.

'So we *did* see right!' said Jack. 'But for that missing tooth, we might never have suspected anything!'

Barbara stopped the film at a moment when the three Djangos were all facing the camera, so that they could have a good look at all three faces.

'They really are identical!' said George. 'Unless it's all clever make-up. I don't see how it's done.'

'Triplets,' said Colin. 'That's how it's done! There's no great mystery about identical triplets.'

'Look – the one on the right has a mole under his left eye,' said Janet. She had moved closer to the screen to get a better view.

'I think the real Django's eyes are the greenest,' said George.

'So do I!' Pam agreed. 'His brothers' eyes aren't so unusual – there's more of a sort of blue shade in them.'

But apart from a slight difference in the colour of their eyes, the mole and the missing tooth, the Seven couldn't find any way at all to tell the triplets apart!

Barbara started the projector again and ran through the rest of the film. Then George pulled the curtain back from the window to let daylight in.

'Oh no!' he exclaimed.

There were Susie and Binkie the other side of the window, looking at him and making faces through the glass!

'Those two horrid girls!' said Peter angrily. 'Why on earth won't they leave us alone?'

Jack was furious too! He got up and marched over to the window.

'You're jolly lucky this window doesn't open, Susie!' he shouted. 'Or I'd lean out and box your ears for you!'

That just made the two little girls laugh.

'Yah boo! We know Django!' they said. They went on and on saying it, making it into a kind of chant. 'We know Django, yah boo! We know Django, sucks to you!'

'Oh, honestly!' said Barbara, feeling exasperated. 'What will they go making up next?'

'We know Django, yah boo! We know Django, sucks to you!'

'That's enough of that!' said Peter sternly. 'Susie, Binkie, tell me what you know about Django! And hurry up about it!'

'We know where Django lives, ya boo! We know where Django lives, so sucks to you!' said the two little pests, going on with their maddening chant.

'They're telling lies!' said Jack.

'We can't be sure of that,' Colin told him.

'Then where *does* he live?' Peter asked the two little girls. Their noses were flattened against the glass of the window-pane!

'Wouldn't you like to know?' said Susie. Binkie laughed. 'I tell you what,' Susie went on. 'We'll tell you where if you'll let us be in your Secret Seven Society.'

'Well, we won't!' said Jack. 'And if you others go and let them join, I'm leaving the Society!'

Janet couldn't help smiling at that.

'Where does Django live?' Peter repeated.

'Will you or won't you let us join your Society?'

This was a difficult situation for Peter. If Susie and Binkie really *did* know where Django lived, he had to get the information out of them somehow. On the other hand, they couldn't possibly be allowed to join the Secret Seven!

'Look, you could come to one or two of our meetings, if you like,' he suggested.

'No!' said Susie very firmly. 'We'll be full members of the Secret Seven or nothing!'

Was Peter going to give in to Susie's blackmail? The other six children held their breath.

'Nothing it is, then!' said Peter. 'If you won't tell us where Django is, we'll just have to find out for ourselves! There's no special hurry. We can take our time about it.'

'Oh no, you can't!' said Binkie triumphantly. 'Because the Big Wheel's left — so there!'

But of course that gave the game away.

'You silly little chatterbox!' Susie said furiously to her friend. 'I've never met anybody so stupid in all my life!'

'Thanks very much for the information, Binkie!' said Jack, grinning.

And the Seven burst out laughing! It really was a funny sight to see those two little pests on the other side of the window – Binkie shedding tears of rage at having been so silly, while Susie made the most horrible faces at her.

Five minutes later, as the Seven left Peter and Janet's garden, they saw Susie and Binkie turning the corner of the road. Obviously they hadn't got the heart to go on following the Seven any more!

'I see it all now!' said Colin. 'It fits together just like a jigsaw. Django is one of the fairground folk who have been here on the Common for the last four weeks. *That's* why the candy floss seller knew him so well!'

'And that's how he managed to get the Big Wheel to stop for him!' said Jack.

'And that's why he was always whistling the fairground music!' Peter added.

The Seven were in a hurry now, and they soon reached the Common, where the fair had been standing until a few days ago. But all they saw there now was a lot of litter, and bits of paper blowing about in the wind. Binkie had warned them, of course, but it was still a disappointment. There were just a few of the fairground people left, taking down the last of the stalls and knocking pegs out of the ground with their big mallets.

'We're too late!' sighed Pam. 'We'll never see Django again.'

'Oh yes, we will!' said Colin grimly. 'And then we'll teach him a lesson!'

Peter went up to one of the fairground men. 'Excuse me,' he said. 'Do you know the Papiropescos?'

'Oh, the family that runs the Big Wheel?' said the man, stopping work for a moment. 'Why, yes. They left the day before yesterday!'

'Do you by any chance know where they were going?' asked Jack.

'To Castleford, I reckon. They planned to be there about a fortnight.'

'Oh, thank you very much, sir,' said Pam. 'That's very kind of you.'

They were just about to walk away again when Colin turned back to the men.

'The Papiropescos have triplets, don't they?' he asked.

'So I'm told!' said the man, grinning. 'But I've never seen all three at once – and they're so much alike, you never know which one you *are* seeing.'

'Thanks,' said Colin, and he joined his friends, smiling broadly. One by one, all his theories were being proved right.

All the Seven had to do now was go to Castleford!

Chapter Thirteen

IN CASTLEFORD

Castleford was a large town about an hour's drive away. A bus passing through the village went there every Saturday morning, and when they counted up the money in their treasury, the Seven found that they had enough for bus tickets for all of them. And there would still be money left over for what they were planning to do when they got to Castleford.

It was going to be a nice day out for them! They didn't mind getting up early to catch the bus – the trip would be fun. Pam had brought a big packet of sandwiches, and George had some lemon squash mixed up in a large plastic bottle.

There were meadows full of flowers and shady woods along the roadside almost all the way to Castleford, and the Seven were enjoying looking out of the bus windows so much that they almost forgot the reason for their trip. At last they arrived – and then they remembered Django.

There was no need to ask their way to the fairground. They saw big red notices up in the streets of Castleford, pointing the way to the fair. But it was

still quite early, and the children guessed that the fair wouldn't be in full swing until the afternoon, so they decided to look round the town.

Jack had been there before, so he was their guide. Castleford was a very interesting old town, with lots of historical buildings, and a museum. The Seven went into the museum to look at the exhibits, and when they came out again it was time for lunch.

They climbed the hill where the old castle that gave the place its name stood, sat on benches, and ate their sandwiches. There was a wonderful view. They could see all the rooftops of the houses, and the church spires of the town, spread out beneath them. And there, in the distance, were tents and colourful flags flying – the fairground! They thought they could see the Big Wheel towering above everything else in the fair.

At two o'clock they decided it was time to set off. They put the wrappings from their sandwiches into a litter-bin and climbed down the Castle Hill again. As they reached the entrance to the fairground, Peter reminded his friends of their plan.

'Remember, you mustn't say anything that would give the game away! And don't let Django see you too soon. I'm sure we can keep the pretence up. After all, we're only going to pretend for about an hour, and Django pretended for four whole weeks!'

'Don't worry, you can rely on us!' Colin told the head of the Seven. 'I'm going to enjoy this!'

And the children set off, mingling with the crowd and making for the Big Wheel.

What *was* their plan? What did Peter mean about pretending? Were they going to play a trick on Django, to pay him back for lying to them?

When they got close to the Big Wheel, they stopped.

'Look!' said Peter. 'There's Django selling the tickets.'

'No, he isn't,' said Barbara. 'He's over there helping customers get into the little cars.'

'No, he isn't,' said George. '*I* can see him just coming out of the machinery part underneath the Big Wheel with an oil can in his hand.'

'Triplets, just as we thought!' said Pam.

There couldn't have been any clearer proof of the way Django had worked his magic tricks.

'Right, I'll go first,' said Peter. 'And the rest of you follow me at intervals.'

He walked away from his friends and went up to the Big Wheel. When he stopped to buy a ticket, he recognised Django – at least, he thought so! Was it really Django or one of his brothers? Were his eyes bright green, or was there a hint of blue in them? Did he or did he not have one tooth missing?

His questions were soon answered, because Django cried, 'Hallo, Peter! Gosh – how nice to see you!'

'What?' said Peter. 'Sorry, my name isn't Peter, and I'm sure I've never met you before!'

'Yes, you have!' said Django. 'Of course you have! You *must* be Peter! I mean, we were at school together in your village only a few days ago!'

'Village?' said Peter, looking blank. 'Sorry, you're wrong again! My name's Jim Smith, and I don't live in a village, I live here in Castleford. Now, can I have a ticket for the Big Wheel, please?'

Django's jaw dropped! But a queue was forming behind Peter, so he couldn't stop to argue. He gave Peter a ticket and his change.

Peter got into one of the cars on the Big Wheel. He had an idea Django Number Two recognised him as he shut the door of the little car, but next moment the Wheel had started to turn and Peter was rising in the air, so neither of them had time to say anything.

Django was still sitting in the ticket office – and he gave a gasp of surprise when he saw Jack and Barbara coming towards him. *They* looked at him as if they didn't recognise him either.

'Two tickets for the Big Wheel, please,' said Jack.

'Listen, you can have a *free* ride!' said Django. 'Only do stop trying to make out you don't know me!'

'Whatever do you mean?' said Barbara, sounding puzzled.

'Stop acting like this – please!' cried Django. 'Jack – won't you stop it?'

'I don't understand a word you're saying!' said Jack. 'Acting like what? Who is this Jack you're talking about?'

Django felt as if his head was going round and round!

'Barbara!' he appealed. 'Surely you're not going to deny you're Barbara?'

'I say, how funny!' said Jack, and he burst out laughing. 'You've got a new name now, have you, Cathy? Well, come on, let's go and have a ride on something else. We don't want to hang around talking to a boy who's off his head!'

Jack and Barbara walked off, arm in arm. Feeling utterly baffled, Django watched them go.

Peter was watching everything as he went round on the Big Wheel. When his car got to the top of the Wheel he saw George, Janet, Pam and Colin on their way towards Django, and a broad smile crossed his face.

'Four tickets, please!' Colin told Django, slapping the money down on the cash desk in front of him.

'Now look, this is going too far!' said Django. 'You're not going to fool me seven times running, so you needn't think you will! All right, maybe I wasn't absolutely honest and truthful, but you see, it was the only way I could . . .'

'What *are* you talking about?' Colin interrupted. He raised his eyebrows, 'Look here, I want to buy four tickets for the Big Wheel!'

'Oh no – this is just too much!' said Django angrily. 'You're pretending too! And now I suppose you're going to say your name isn't Colin, and the others aren't Janet and George and Pam!'

'He's mad!' said Colin.

'Stark, staring mad!' agreed George.

'Stop fooling about, or I won't give you your tickets!' said Django.

'Oh, won't you, though? We'll see about that!' said Colin, and he leaned over and grabbed Django by the collar of his blue boiler suit.

At that there was a growl – and a golden spaniel

came bounding out of the ticket office, baring his teeth at Colin. The spaniel was very like Scamper, except that he had a pink nose instead of a black one, and a white marking like a crescent moon between his eyes . . .

'Don't!' said Pam. 'Oh, do stop it, both of you!'

'At least *you* seem to be feeling more sensible, Pam!' said Django. But Colin kept hold of him, although the dog was yapping round his ankles.

Then Peter came up. He had just finished his ride on the Big Wheel. 'All right, let him go!' he told Colin.

Colin did as Peter said, and they all turned round and marched away from the Big Wheel without another word. Not far off, they met Jack and Barbara.

'Please — don't go!' Django called after them. 'Come back! You're my *friends*, aren't you? Honestly, I can explain it all!'

Pam turned round. There was such a pleading look in Django's eyes! She simply couldn't help it — she turned and ran back to the Big Wheel.

'Pam, come here!' Peter shouted after her.

'Oh no! She'll ruin everything!' said Colin furiously.

Chapter Fourteen

A HAPPY ENDING

But Pam hadn't ruined anything! It was just the opposite!

A few days later Peter had called another meeting of the Secret Seven, and everyone was waiting for Pam.

'Late as usual!' said Colin.

'Goodness knows we ought to be used to *that* by now!' said Jack.

'Ssh! I hear footsteps,' said Peter, and a moment later there was a knock at the door of the shed.

'Password?' asked Peter.

'Triplets!' said Pam, and she giggled. The others couldn't think why. 'Triplets' was their password for the meeting, that was all!

But when Peter opened the door, they were astonished to see that there *were* triplets outside! Pam was there – accompanied by all three Djangos!

'You traitor!' said Colin angrily.

'I'm not a traitor,' Pam snapped. 'Colin, if you'd talked to Django you'd have understood everything a lot better. Well, I *have* talked to him – and here he is with his brothers Ivan and Sasha, and they want to apologise!'

'All right. They can come in,' Peter agreed.

Pam beamed. She showed the triplets where they could sit, and sat down on a box beside them.

'As Pam told you, we've come to say we're sorry,' Django began. 'It's quite true, we *did* take advantage of your trusting natures. We're none of us really magicians. But you see, I thought if I pretended to be someone a bit special, I'd make friends with you sooner. You wouldn't have been so interested if I'd seemed to be just an ordinary boy. It might have taken us months to get to know each other, and I never *stay* anywhere for months!'

'That's right,' put in Ivan, one of the brothers. 'When you're moving around from fairground to fairground, you're never anywhere for long enough to make real friends. That's not much fun. It's lucky for us that we're triplets, and we get on well together.'

'And you can pretend to be each other if you want to, as well,' said Colin.

He actually sounded friendly! The Papiropesco triplets had convinced him that they didn't mean any harm. Pam could tell from his tone of voice, and she was very glad indeed. It was all her doing!

The other five were happy to accept apologies from Django, Sasha and Ivan. But there were still a few questions they wanted to ask.

'Why didn't you all three come to our school?' said Peter. 'Having triplets in the class would have been interesting all right!'

'It's because of the subjects we're learning, especially modern languages,' Django explained. 'You see, travelling round as we do in our family, it's a very good thing to be able to speak foreign languages, so our parents are very keen for us to learn them. Well – Sasha and Ivan are learning French and Spanish, and I'm learning French and German. Those are the languages they teach at your school, Peter, but they don't teach any Spanish, so my brothers had to go to school in Covelty, where they *do* have Spanish lessons!'

'There wasn't much risk of meeting you,' Ivan explained, 'because Covelty is quite a long way away from this village.'

'How did my awful little sister Susie and her friend get to know about you?' asked Jack.

'That was sheer bad luck,' said Sasha. 'You see, they came to the fair one day and recognised Django selling tickets for the Big Wheel.'

'They'd already seen me at Scamper's birthday party!' Django explained.

'And we had to give them no end of free rides on the Big Wheel so that they'd promise not to tell you anything about us,' Ivan said.

'Honestly, those girls are dreadful! They certainly know how to blackmail people,' said George. 'They wouldn't have told us about you anyway – they were only too pleased to see you playing a trick on us!'

Just then Scamper woke up. He had been sleeping

at Peter's feet. When he saw the triplets he sat there looking absolutely baffled! Which of these three boys was the one who had shut him up in that trunk?

The spaniel sniffed the three brothers one by one. It seemed as if he couldn't make up his mind.

'I ought to apologise to you too, Scamper!' said Django. 'You didn't like it much inside the trunk, did you? I couldn't have brought that trick off if we didn't have a spaniel of our own who's rather like you.'

'He's a lovely dog, too!' said Pam. 'His name is Signor Piero, and he's a genuine performing dog.'

'Yes, but he was terribly puzzled when I called him Signor *Scam*piero. He usually reacts at once, but this time it took him a few moments to realise I meant him.'

'Did the trunk have a false bottom?' asked Janet.

'Yes,' said Django. 'I could make either Scamper or Signor Piero come out – and a little stage make-up helped my trick too.'

'So *that's* why Scamper kept sniffing the trunk!' said Peter. 'He knew Signor Piero was inside.'

'Now then, Scamper, Django's apologised to you – so be a good sport and shake paws,' Pam said. And the good dog did as she asked, putting out a paw to one of the triplets.

'No, Scamper – Django, not Sasha!' Barbara told him.

'Sorry,' said another of the triplets, 'but *I'm* Sasha! He's Ivan!'

'Oh no, he's not!' said the third triplet. 'Stop

fooling about, Django! Listen, I'm Sasha, he's Ivan, and he's Django!'

'You're just trying to get them all mixed up!' said the first triplet. 'I'm Django, he's Sasha and he's Ivan!'

And everybody collapsed into laughter! As the Secret Seven all agreed, Django and his brothers really did have a kind of magic of their own, even if it wasn't exactly what the children had expected — because looking from one triplet to the other and then the other, it was next to impossible for anyone to tell them apart . . .

If you have enjoyed this book, you may like to
read some more exciting adventures
from Knight Books:

A complete list of new adventures about the SECRET SEVEN

KNIGHT BOOKS

A complete list of the SECRET SEVEN ADVENTURES by Enid Blyton

KNIGHT BOOKS

A complete list of the FAMOUS FIVE ADVENTURES by Enid Blyton

1. FIVE ON A TREASURE ISLAND
2. FIVE GO ADVENTURING AGAIN
3. FIVE RUN AWAY TOGETHER
4. FIVE GO TO SMUGGLER'S TOP
5. FIVE GO OFF IN A CARAVAN
6. FIVE ON KIRRIN ISLAND AGAIN
7. FIVE GO OFF TO CAMP
8. FIVE GET INTO TROUBLE
9. FIVE FALL INTO ADVENTURE
10. FIVE ON A HIKE TOGETHER
11. FIVE HAVE A WONDERFUL TIME
12. FIVE GO DOWN TO THE SEA
13. FIVE GO TO MYSTERY MOOR
14. FIVE HAVE PLENTY OF FUN
15. FIVE ON A SECRET TRAIL
16. FIVE GO TO BILLYCOCK HILL
17. FIVE GET INTO A FIX
18. FIVE ON FINNISTON FARM
19. FIVE GO TO DEMON'S ROCKS
20. FIVE HAVE A MYSTERY TO SOLVE
21. FIVE ARE TOGETHER AGAIN

KNIGHT BOOKS

A complete list of new adventures about the FAMOUS FIVE

KNIGHT BOOKS

A list of stories about the
GUMBY GANG by Pamela Oldfield

THE ADVENTURES OF THE GUMBY GANG
MORE ABOUT THE GUMBY GANG
THE GUMBY GANG STRIKES AGAIN

KNIGHT BOOKS